My Family

Dad

Mum

my sister, the Witch Baby

# Oliver Moon
## and the
# Spider Spell

## Sue Mongredien

### Illustrated by
## Jan McCafferty

USBORNE

For Hannah Powell,
who had lots of great ideas for this story.

First published in 2008 by Usborne Publishing Ltd., Usborne House,
83-85 Saffron Hill, London EC1N 8RT, England. www.usborne.com

Text copyright © Sue Mongredien Ltd., 2008

Illustration copyright © Usborne Publishing Ltd., 2008

A CIP catalogue record for this book is available from
the British Library.

J MAMJJASOND/08    ISBN 9780746090749

Printed in Great Britain.

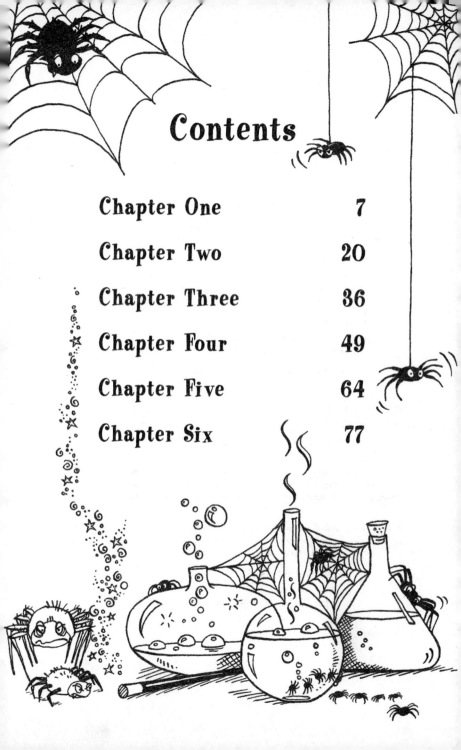

# Contents

**Chapter One**

Oliver Moon opened his eyes and sat up in his spiderweb hammock, yawning and stretching. Then he smiled. It was Saturday today – the best day of the week. No Magic School, no lessons, no bossy teachers…just lots of fun doing whatever he felt like.

Maybe he'd phone his best friend Jake

Frogfreckle and they'd play skull football in the park.

Maybe they'd go pond-dipping with their fishing nets. The last time they'd done that, Oliver had caught a real nettle-newt and seventeen sludge-snails.

Or maybe, if it was raining, Oliver could make cockroach cookies with his parents. Yum!

Oliver got out of bed, his mind spinning with ideas. Oh, how he loved Saturdays! He pulled on his dressing gown and ran downstairs for breakfast.

In the kitchen, he stopped and stared at the scene of chaos that greeted him. The Witch Baby, Oliver's little sister, had just put her bowl of beetle-crunch cereal on her head, and streams of bat milk

were running down her face and hair.
"Hee hee! Look at me!" she chirruped
cheerfully.

Meanwhile, Oliver's dad, Mr. Moon,
was standing on a chair, wiping
splattered baby food off the ceiling.
"Oliver, thank goodness you're awake!"
he cried. "Madam here is being very
messy this morning, and—" He broke off

as he turned and caught sight of his daughter with cereal and milk all over her head. "What have you done *now?*" he said with a sigh.

"Me MORE messy!" the Witch Baby replied with a big grin.

Mr. Moon looked worn out. "Honestly, I don't know how your mum manages it," he said to Oliver. Then he grabbed a cloth and went over to the Witch Baby. "Let's clean you up," he said wearily. "Then it's time for your vitamins."

"YUCK!" said the Witch Baby as he wiped a wet flannel over her face.

Mr. Moon got a bottle of treacly-looking black liquid from the cupboard and poured some onto a spoon. "Open wide!" he told her.

The Witch Baby shook her head, her lips clamped together.

"I said—" Mr. Moon began, but Oliver interrupted.

"She won't have it like that," he whispered. "Mum sneaks it onto a biscuit, so that she doesn't know she's swallowing it." He looked around. "Where *is* Mum anyway?" he asked.

"She's not very well," Mr. Moon replied, opening the biscuit tin. "She's got a nasty case of the green flu, so—"

"Green flu?" Oliver echoed. "Is that where you turn green?"

Mr. Moon nodded. "Bright frog-green, yes," he said, dribbling the vitamin liquid onto a beetle biscuit. "Even her hair is green. And her teeth. She feels awful, poor thing. She'll have to stay in bed until she's better. Green flu takes a while to recover from. Which means there are a few chores we'll have to share today, Oliver. And of course your sister needs looking after."

Oliver's heart sank. Chores? Looking after his sister? On a *Saturday*? "But..." he began.

"Who wants a yummy scrummy bicky, then?" Mr. Moon asked the Witch Baby, and she opened her mouth wide at once. "Brilliant, Ol," he said, as he posted the beetle biscuit in.

"Now, there's a list of chores here," he went on, passing a piece of paper over. "As you'll see, I've divided the work up between us, so…"

Oliver scanned through the list, tuning out his dad's voice as he did so.

*Putting away breakfast things — Oliver*
*Washing cloaks — Oliver*
*Recharging wands — Oliver*
*Looking after the Witch Baby — Oliver*
*Taking cauldron for servicing — Dad*

Oliver gaped as he read. Chore after chore after chore — and nearly all with his name on them! Suddenly, his plans for pond-dipping and skull football seemed a million miles away. "That's not fair! I've got to do everything!" he complained.

Mr. Moon shrugged. "Ahh, but it'll take a while to get the cauldron serviced," he replied. "You know what they're like at Kwik-Fix. I could be there hours! And it must be done today, too. It's been booked in for ages, and if I cancel we'll have to wait months before we can get it seen again."

"Well, can't you take the Witch Baby with you?" Oliver suggested.

They both turned to look at the Witch Baby, who was now trying to wedge her cereal spoon up her nose.

Mr. Moon yanked it out, causing her to break into howls of dismay.

"No, sorry," Mr. Moon told Oliver. "You know what she's like. She'll meddle with everything, and trash the place. It's just not possible. She'll be much better off here with you. Now, I'd better get the cauldron and go on my way. I'll be as quick as I can."

"What — that's it? You're leaving me in charge, just like that?" Oliver asked.

"Juss like dat, juss like dat," the Witch Baby chanted. She had the annoying habit of copying everything Oliver and his parents said at the moment; it was her new game.

"I'll be back as soon as I can," Mr. Moon said. "Mum's upstairs if you really need her. Oh, and try to keep your sister quiet. You know we'll only have Mrs. B next door complaining if she makes a racket. The last thing we want is that old grouch — I mean—" He

clapped his hand
over his mouth.
"I didn't say that,
all right?"

Oliver grinned,
despite himself.
He knew his dad
wasn't very
keen on Mrs.
Beardbristle, the
Moons' neighbour. Mind you, neither was
Oliver. She was the most bad-tempered,
mean old witch he'd ever met. "See you
later, then, Dad," he said.

He sighed as he went to the kitchen to
make some batwing toast. To think that,
just a few minutes ago, he'd been looking
forward to today. Now he was starting

to wish he was at school. Anything would be more exciting than chores and babysitting!

Chapter Two

After breakfast, Oliver left his sister playing with her spooky magnets on the fridge, and went up to see his mum.

"Yes?" came a feeble voice when he knocked on the bedroom door.

Oliver went in, and gasped at the sight of his mum in bed, her face and hair grass-green, her eyes dull and tired-looking. He felt really guilty about complaining to Dad about the chores now. He had never seen his mum look so ill!

"Hi, Mum," he said. "Um… Do you want any breakfast? A cup of cockroach coffee?"

Mrs. Moon coughed loudly, making the bed shake. "A glass of pond water, please," she said in a weak voice. "And a slice of prickleberry pie would be nice, too. Thank you. You're such a good boy, Oliver." She sneezed three times and shut her eyes.

"Okay," Oliver replied. He ran out to the garden and filled a glass with murky brown pond water, then went to get some of the pie. Dad had cooked it for tea yesterday, and Oliver had noticed there was a slice left in the fridge. But when he went into the kitchen, he saw the fridge door was wide open – and his sister was busily emptying the contents!

"Yum yum! Me have MORE breakfast!" she said when Oliver ran over.

She had toad jam all over her face and
her fingertips were bright purple.
And…oh, no! What was that, smeared
all over the floor?

"You've wrecked the last slice of pie!"
Oliver cried in dismay. She seemed to
have trodden on it, as there were

prickleberries oozing between her toes, and bits of pastry squidged on the tiles.

"Wrecked the pie," his sister agreed.

 She scooped a berry from under her big toe and offered it to Oliver. "You like?"

"No!" he snapped. "I don't like!

Mum wanted this for her breakfast and now you've ruined it."

"Ruined it," the Witch Baby echoed thoughtfully. Then she carefully peeled a strip of pastry from the sole of her foot. "Me give this to Mum," she said kindly. "*She* like."

"No," Oliver sighed. "She not like." He looked in despair from his sister to the glass of pond water. "Look, stay there," he ordered. "I'm going to take Mum her drink. And then I'm going to clean you up. All right?"

"Clean you up," his sister sang, lying down and rolling in the prickleberry mess. "All right."

Oliver gritted his teeth as he left the room. He hoped Dad would come home soon! His sister was proving hard work already – and he'd only just started looking after her.

Upstairs, he carefully set the glass of pond water on his mum's bedside table. "Here's your water," he told her. "And… there's been a bit of a problem with the pie. Could I get you anything else?"

His mum's face fell in disappointment. "Oh," she said. "That's a shame. I did really fancy the pie." She blew her nose loudly and sighed. "Never mind. Thanks for the water."

Oliver tiptoed out of the room as his mum closed her eyes and seemed to go to sleep. Maybe he could make her a new pie! Yes – that would cheer her up, wouldn't it? There were loads of prickleberries in the cupboard. He could stew some up in the cauldron…

Ahh. No, he couldn't. Dad had taken the cauldron in to be serviced, hadn't he?

Oliver sat on the bottom of the stairs, thinking. Did he dare go next door and ask Mrs. Beardbristle if he could borrow *her* cauldron? She was such a dragon, she would probably shout something horrible at him and slam the door in his face. But maybe, just maybe, if he was really polite and explained about Mum being ill and wanting to make a pie for her, then there was a chance she'd help out. Surely not even Mrs. Beardbristle could say no to that!

\*

"Let's sort you out then," Oliver said to his sister, after he'd cleared up all the mess on the kitchen floor and set the wands recharging. He led her to her bedroom and took off her pyjamas. Then, pinching his nose, he undid her night-time nappy and cleaned her up.

"Me smelly," she said proudly.

Oliver coughed, his eyes watering. "You certainly are," he said, fanning away the pong. He put a clean nappy on her and some clothes, then took her back downstairs. "Right, come on," he said. "Let's get this over with. Let's go and visit old badger-breath Beardbristle."

He helped his sister on with her shoes, then they went to the house next door. Snakes hissed at them as they approached, and a yellow-eyed cat snarled, showing sharp white teeth.

Oliver pressed the doorbell, which made the sound of a wolf howling. ARROOOOOOO! ARROOOOOOO!

"Coming!" moaned a grumpy voice from inside, and Oliver heard the loud tramp of footsteps. Then the door was flung open, and there stood Mrs. Beardbristle, glaring down at Oliver and his sister, her meaty arms folded over her chest.

"Whadda YOU want?" she snorted. "Ringing my bell for fun, are you? Think it's a joke to disturb me?"

Oliver trembled. "No, I just…I…" His mind had gone blank. He felt transfixed by Mrs. Beardbristle's ferocious scowl. "Um…"

The Witch Baby didn't seem the slightest bit scared, though. "Old badger-breath," she said to Mrs. Beardbristle. "Ollie said. Old badger-breath Beardbristle. Badgery badgery badgery!"

Mrs. Beardbristle's eyes looked as if they were about to pop out. "Of all the nerve!" she shrieked. "Of all the rudeness! Wait till your parents hear about THIS!"

And she slammed the door right in their faces.

"No, wait!" Oliver cried desperately. "Mrs. Badger – I mean, Mrs. Beard-badger, I…" He groaned. "Oh, no!" He opened the letter box. "I'm sorry for what she said," he called through it. "Please may we borrow your cauldron? My mum's ill and—"

But before Oliver could say another word, a bar of soap had shot out of the letter box, straight into his mouth. "Naughty, rude children need their mouths washed out," the soap chanted as it rubbed itself all over Oliver's tongue.

Ugh! Oliver wiped the bubbles from his chin with his cloak as the soap whizzed towards the Witch Baby. "Oh, no you don't!" Oliver said, making a grab for it.

It zoomed right through his fingers, though, and washed out his sister's mouth too, making her cry in dismay.

"And don't come back!" Mrs. Beardbristle boomed from an upstairs window, as the enchanted soap finished its work and flew back up to her. "Nasty little things. Go on! Get away from my house!"

Oliver took his sister's hand and led her home. She was still crying and blowing soap bubbles from her mouth. What a disaster! Now he'd never get the cauldron, and wouldn't be able to make a pie for his mum. And Mrs. Beardbristle was probably already composing a furious Magic Message to blast round to his parents. He was going to be in so much trouble!

*

Back in the house, Oliver left his sister
playing with her pet spider Hairy Horace
and some toys, then went to the kitchen.
The spare cauldron was in the cupboard
but that was no good for berry-stewing –
it was way too small. Then his eye fell
upon his wand, where it sat recharging
in the power-pod,
and he stopped,
his mind racing.
A brilliant
thought had
just struck him.
A brilliant
thought that would solve everything!
Oliver grinned and snatched up his wand.
"Yes!" he whooped. "I am a genius!"

Chapter
Three

Of course! He could magic the spare cauldron bigger! How he wished he'd thought of it earlier – he could have avoided grumpy old Mrs. Beardbristle altogether. Much easier!

He took a couple of spell books off the kitchen shelf and put them on the table. He was sure he'd be able to find a spell or potion that would tell him how to make objects bigger. And then...bingo! Problem solved!

Oliver blew the dust off the first spell book and opened it up. He wasn't supposed to do magic at home without his parents' permission, but he was sure they wouldn't mind this time. They would probably congratulate him on his quick thinking!

"Ollie, me hungry," came a little voice just then, and Oliver turned to see the Witch Baby in the doorway, with Hairy Horace perched on her head. "Me have snack now?"

"You can't be hungry already," Oliver told her. "You've only just had breakfast!" He leafed through the spell book. Let's see… There was a spell to turn your cat into a tiger, a spell to make a frog sing, a spell to turn your feet into wheels, a spell to make your enemy freeze into a giant icicle…

"Only juss, only juss," the Witch Baby

chanted. "Only juss had breakfast."

"Let me do this," Oliver said, turning more pages. "I'll get you a snack in a... Ahh!" He jabbed his finger at the spell book. *Grow-bigger spell*, it said at the top of the page. "Brilliant."

"Bwilliant," the Witch Baby agreed, sitting down on the floor and stroking Hairy Horace.

Oliver read through the words of the spell and clutched his wand. It was quite a complicated spell, written in an old-fashioned magical language, and he wasn't sure how to pronounce all of the words. "Let's give it a go," he muttered to himself. "Okay... Haddle-me, rinkubus..."

"Had a wee, dinky bus," the Witch Baby repeated. "Had a wee, Horace?" she asked, tickling the spider under the chin.

"Hush!" Oliver told her. "Haddle-me, rinkubus, swizzer pong pig…"

"Pongy piggy, pongy piggy," chanted the Witch Baby, pulling all the wands out of the recharging pod and twirling them around. "Me have snack now?"

Oliver couldn't concentrate. How was he supposed to cast this spell with his sister wittering on in the background? "Look, why don't you and Horace go outside for a bit?" he said, still staring down at the book. "Go and play in the garden."

He heard his sister patter out through the back door behind him, then he checked the words of the spell one last time, before pointing his wand at the cauldron. "Haddle-me, rinkubus, swizzer pong pig. My magic makes you really big!" he chanted.

He dimly heard his sister talking to Horace outside, but ignored her. He was too busy watching a stream of fizzling red magic whoosh from the end of his wand and pour over the cauldron. Would the spell work? Had he pronounced all the words right?

There was a scraping sound and the cauldron suddenly flashed a bright electric blue, and then plumes of pink smoke billowed from it.

"Haddle-me, rinkybus, swizzer pong pig…" he heard the Witch Baby giggling from outside.

Ka-boom! There was a loud bang and Oliver jumped back in alarm. Then the pink smoke cleared to reveal the most enormous cauldron Oliver had ever seen, right there in the kitchen.

"I did it!" he cheered. "I actually did it!"

"My magic makes YOU really big!" the Witch Baby chuckled outside. "Ooh, Horace!" he heard her splutter. "Ooooh!"

Oliver clapped his hand against the cauldron and it gave a pleasing metallic clang. Yes – it was real. He'd done it!

Humming to himself, he tipped the boxes of prickleberries into the cauldron, along with several scoops of snail-sugar to stew. There! It wouldn't be long before they were ready to go in a pie.

His mum would be so pleased and, with a bit of luck, it would make her feel much better again.

He turned round to see a couple of wands on the floor, where his sister had been playing with them. Hmmm, one was missing. Had it rolled under the dresser or something?

He bent down to peer under the kitchen dresser and the table, but couldn't spot it anywhere. Then he happened to glance out the back door, and groaned to see his sister clutching the missing wand. He should have known that little monkey would be responsible!

"Haddle-me, rinkybus, swizzer pong pig…" the Witch Baby was cooing, waving the wand above her head.

Oliver stared. What was that enormous black creature beside her? His mouth was dry with horror. "Is that...is that really Hairy Horace?" he croaked.

"Yes, Horace!" the Witch Baby laughed. "He so 'NORMOUS now!"

Oliver's jaw dropped open in shock. Hairy Horace was the size of an elephant, and stood towering over the Moon's garden, peering around beadily with his big black eyes.

"Give me that at once!" Oliver shouted, grabbing the wand out of his sister's hand.

Hairy Horace seemed startled at Oliver's shout and galumphed away down the garden.

"Come back!" the Witch Baby
bellowed, tears springing to her eyes.
"Come back, Horace!"

But Horace didn't seem to like all the
shouting. With one last look at the Witch
Baby and Oliver, he vaulted the garden
fence with his great hairy legs, and
scuttled away.

Chapter
Four

Oliver felt sick with dread as he watched
the gigantic spider rampaging through
Mrs. Beardbristle's garden, trampling all
her strangle-plants as it did so. Then it
went over the far wall and disappeared.

Oliver could hear faint screams in the
distance and wondered if Hairy Horace
had just given someone a nasty shock.

Horace was the most gentle pet you could imagine, but Oliver guessed that if you didn't know him, an elephant-sized spider might seem a bit alarming.

"Hello! I'm back!" came a shout just then, and Oliver froze to the spot. Uh-oh. Now Dad was home. Oliver was going to get in *so* much trouble!

The Witch Baby was still dripping with tears. "Horace GONE!" she wailed as Mr. Moon came out into the garden. "He GONE, Dad!"

"Oh dear," Mr. Moon said mildly. "Never mind, he'll be back. The good news is the cauldron's been serviced and I've picked up some Cure-Alls for your mum." He patted his jacket pocket, looking pleased with himself.

"Er, Dad, the thing is…" Oliver said.
"Horace has…grown a bit. In fact…"

The Witch Baby sniffed and wiped her
nose on her cloak. "He big, Dad," she
said, sounding slightly more cheerful.
"He 'NORMOUS!"

Mr. Moon looked baffled and, with a nervous gulp, Oliver explained everything. "Oh dear," Mr. Moon said. "Oh no. You mean...he's just gone? Which way?"

"That way," Oliver replied, pointing. "Towards town."

"Then there's no time to lose," Mr. Moon said. "Come on, get your broomstick, Oliver. This is an emergency. We need to get Horace home and back to his normal size, before he causes any trouble!"

Seconds later, Oliver, his dad and his sister were flying through the air, in search of Horace. Oliver had packed a tub of Horace's favourite spider food, just in case they could tempt him home with it. Oliver peered over his broomstick, searching for the runaway spider. "What is *that*?" he gasped, pointing down below, where a gleaming silver rope was looped around a house.

Mr. Moon looked grim. "I think that must be spider-silk that Horace has spun, for an enormous web," he replied. "Only it's much thicker now that Horace is so big. Looking on the bright side, we know he definitely went this way!"

Horace certainly had left an easy trail to follow. The thick ropes of silver spider-silk were everywhere – around trees and houses, and across roads. There were also huddles of frightened people clutching one another or trying to cut through the silk.

"Once we get close to him, we'll need to catch him before we can shrink him," Mr. Moon called across to Oliver. "We can't send spells whizzing all over the place in the hope that one will hit him. Any ideas how we can catch him?"

Oliver shook his head. He hadn't thought about that. "I don't know," he replied. "Lasso him?"

They were flying over a large garden with a washing line full of clean cloaks just then. Mr. Moon flew down, thrust his wand out and chanted:

*"Take down the washing and fold it up fine*
*We need to borrow that washing line!"*

Red crackles came from the end of his wand, and the clothes on the line magically unpegged themselves and flew into a neat pile on the lawn. The washing line then untied itself and soared right into Mr. Moon's hand. "A lasso is a great idea, Oliver," Mr. Moon said.

"We can catch him, then find some kind of Shrinking spell to use on him." He gave a gasp suddenly. "Oh my word! Is that him?"

Oliver stared ahead, where they could see a massive black creature leaping over the fields. "That's him, all right," he replied.

"Ooh, Horace, come here!" the Witch Baby squeaked, from where she was strapped in behind Mr. Moon. "Bad Horace, come back!"

Mr. Moon tied a loop in one end of the washing line to make a lasso, then swung it round his head a few times, cowboy-style. Then, as they swooped nearer to Horace, he flung the lasso out...and it fell right over the spider's huge hairy head!

"Yay, Dad!" Oliver cheered, clapping
his hands and almost tumbling off his
broomstick in excitement.

But their feelings of triumph didn't last
long. With a great chomp of his gigantic
jaws, Horace had bitten through the
washing line, and was off on the run once
more, crossing the wide River Sludge with
a leap of his long, hairy legs. He seemed to
be having a great time, being enormous.

There were a couple of fisher-witches down on the banks of the river. Seeing their nets gave Oliver another idea. "How about using a net, to try and trap him?" he bellowed over to his dad.

Mr. Moon nodded and gave him a thumbs-up. "Good thinking, Ol," he replied. "Let's see what my wand can do this time." He gripped it firmly and pointed it at Horace.

*"String and twine I need to get*
*To magic up a mighty net!"*

Oliver watched expectantly, but there
was only the smallest of crackles from
Mr. Moon's wand – and then a titchy,
mouse-sized net appeared in the air with
a feeble puff of smoke.

"Oh, no!" Oliver groaned, realizing too late what the problem was. "Your wand didn't finish recharging, Dad. The Witch Baby took them all out of the pod to play with. And now the power's all gone!" Oliver gave his own wand a shake, but it too emitted just the faintest of crackles. He must have used up all its power when he'd cast the Grow-bigger spell.

Mr. Moon looked stricken at this news, and Oliver felt a lurch of panic. Two powerless wands and a gigantic runaway spider... However would they be able to catch Horace now?

## Chapter Five

They had reached the centre of Cacklewick by this point, and as they soared in over the shops and houses, they saw that Horace had clambered up the roof of the Town Hall and was weaving more silver ropes of silk.

"What he DOING?" the Witch Baby asked, wide-eyed, as they flew down to land.

"He's spinning a web," Oliver replied, watching Horace. "All over the Town Hall!"

There was a crowd of people gathered in the town square staring up in horror at Horace as he busily spun his silk from the rooftops. The silk was bound round and round the windows of the top floor of the Town Hall, and Oliver watched in dismay as people inside the buildings tried to open their windows but found them completely stuck.

"What is that spider-monster? Where did it come from?" people were asking nervously. "How can we get rid of it?"

The Witch Baby looked alarmed. "Not get rid of Horace!" she cried. "He MINE!"

"He's harmless!" Mr. Moon shouted

out. "We just need to find a way of shrinking him, that's all. Don't hurt him!"

Nobody seemed to be listening in all the kerfuffle. Wands were raised at Horace, and Oliver heard a number of Zap and Freezing spells being chanted.

Sparks and crackles and streams
of magic hurtled towards Horace, but
he dodged behind the web, missing all
of them. Even worse, the magic spells
rebounded off the web, and started
striking innocent witches and wizards
down below.

Zap! An old witch was stunned and fell over backwards. Luckily, she was caught by a group of other witches just before she hit the ground.

Flash! A wizard on a bicycle was frozen to the spot, like a statue. Oliver stared in amazement as a bird landed on his head, as if it were a perch.

"Stop your spells!" cried a tall wizard with a long grey beard and a gold chain, dressed in purple robes, who'd just battled his way out of the Town Hall. "They are making things even worse!"

"It's the mayor," Mr. Moon whispered. "Let's hope he can sort this mess out."

The mayor tapped the stunned witch and the frozen wizard with a silver wand, and they turned back to normal. Then he stared around at the crowd. "Who is responsible for this creature?" he boomed.

Oliver swallowed hard. "Er..." he began nervously.

"He MINE," the Witch Baby said proudly. "He Hairy Horace. I make him BIG!"

Everyone turned to stare at Oliver's little sister, standing there looking very pleased with herself.

"I might have known," came a sarcastic voice from the crowd, and Oliver blushed to see Mrs. Beardbristle glaring at them in disapproval.

The mayor didn't seem to have heard her, luckily. "You made him big, did you?" he asked the Witch Baby. "All on your own?"

"We're really sorry," Oliver said,

hanging his head. "She used the Grow-bigger spell, and it was kind of my fault because—"

"It was my fault," Mr. Moon said staunchly. "I left them on their own and…"

"What a family! They're all as bad as each other," Mrs. Beardbristle muttered.

The mayor looked up at Horace, and down at the Witch Baby. "Well, a Reverse spell won't work," he said. "Not while he's using that web as a shield. We'll have to give him an antidote. Hold on!" And he dashed into a nearby Spell Supplies shop.

By now, Horace had spun his spider-silk all around the Town Hall, completely sealing the building. Lots of passers-by

had been tangled up in the sticky web
and were calling out
for help.

"You should be ashamed of yourselves!" Mrs. Beardbristle shouted to Mr. Moon, her arms folded across her chest. "Honestly! What a mess! Those children of yours need a good punishment for this."

Oliver felt his cheeks smart at her words, but Mr. Moon put a hand on his shoulder. "Just ignore her," he whispered. "Don't listen to the old grouch. It was an accident."

"Here!" cried the mayor just then, rushing back with a purple pill the size of a dinner plate. "Had to get an extra-large, just because the spider is so big!" He handed it to Mr. Moon. "There – do you think you can persuade that beast to eat it?"

Mr. Moon gulped nervously. "I'll give it a go," he replied. "Look after your sister," he told Oliver.

Oliver and the Witch Baby watched as Mr. Moon kicked his broomstick off the ground and zoomed up towards Horace, holding the pill out in front of him. Everyone in the crowd held their breath and watched as Mr. Moon flew nearer and nearer the huge black spider. "Here, Horace," Oliver could hear his dad shouting. "Eat this up, there's a good boy…"

Horace scuttled back from the pill, looking at it in disgust, and shaking his big head.

Mr. Moon tried again, flying a little closer, his arm outstretched. "Come on, Horace," he shouted. "It's delicious! Just give it a try…"

But Horace wasn't having any of it. He just scurried further away on the roof, making a leap to the next building along.

There was a groan of disappointment from the crowd. "He's not falling for that one," Oliver heard someone sigh.

"Horace, he say yuck," the Witch Baby commented, watching.

Oliver nodded. "Just like you and your vitamins," he said – and then he had an idea. "Hey!" he cried. "That's it! That's the answer!"

## Chapter Six

The mayor – and lots of members of the crowd – all turned at Oliver's shout.

"What's the answer?" the mayor asked.

Beaming, Oliver told them what had happened with his sister and the vitamins that morning. "When Dad tried to give them to her on a spoon, she wouldn't open her mouth," he explained. "But as soon as he put the vitamin liquid on a biscuit, she gobbled it up."

"Gobble gobble," the Witch Baby agreed.

"But what does this have to do with the spider?" the mayor asked, confused.

"It's the same thing," Oliver told him. "While we're trying to give Horace something he doesn't like the look of, he's not going to eat it. But if we disguise the pill in something Horace *will* eat..."

"Brilliant!" the mayor cried, and there was a buzz of admiration from the crowd.

"What a clever little wizard!" Oliver heard someone say.

Mr. Moon landed just then, looking disappointed. "He wouldn't even try it," he said, his shoulders slumped.

"Don't worry, Dad, we've had an idea," Oliver said. He pulled out the tub of spider food from his pocket. "If we stick this all over the antidote pill, Horace might give it a try."

Mr. Moon clapped him on the back. "Great thinking, Oliver!" he cried. "Let's do it."

A few minutes later, the purple pill looked like a huge slab of spider food, covered in dried flies and insects.

Oliver took a deep breath. "I'll take it up to him," he offered. "He might be suspicious if you go again, Dad."

"Are you sure?" Mr. Moon asked. "It's quite tricky, steering the broomstick and holding that big pill at the same time, you know."

"Perhaps I should try," the mayor volunteered, with a wary glance at Horace.

Oliver put a leg over his broomstick. "No, I'll go," he said. "He knows me. And besides, I got us into this mess – so I'll get us out of it."

"Good luck!" Mr. Moon said, clapping him on the back.

Oliver kicked off into the air, the pill tucked under one arm. Horace was now making a thick web between the Town Hall and the shopping centre and several unsuspecting witches and wizards had already flown straight into it on their broomsticks, getting completely stuck.

Oliver's heart pounded as he approached Horace. The closer he got, the more intimidated he felt by the sheer size of his sister's pet.

Horace's legs were as long as tree trunks. His jaws were worryingly big and sharp-looking. And his eyes were scarily beady, as if they could see right into Oliver's mind.

Oliver's hands trembled as he steered
the broomstick nearer the web. He was
aware of a hushed silence below as
everyone watched. He had to get this
right. He had to make things okay again!

"Here goes," he muttered, and held out
the fly-covered pill so that Horace could

see it. "Horace, it's me, Oliver," he called softly. "I've brought you some yummy food. I thought you might be hungry."

Horace stared at the pill, unblinking. Then he looked at Oliver.

"I'll leave it just here for you," Oliver said, putting it carefully on a corner of the web. "And when you get hungry, you can come and eat it. Okay?"

Oliver backed away slowly on his broomstick, hoping with all his heart that Horace was peckish after his silk-spinning. "Any time you want, Horace," he said, trying to sound encouraging. Inside, though, he was starting to worry. Why wasn't Horace coming over? Had he guessed it was a trick?

He waited for a few moments, but he was fast losing hope. It wasn't going to work, was it? Just another of his stupid ideas, like magicking the cauldron bigger. Why had he ever thought this was a good plan?

He turned to fly back down, his spirits sinking. "Sorry, everyone," he called.

"I guess it didn't—"

But nobody was looking at him. Everyone's eyes were fixed on a point just behind him. And then, all of a sudden, there was a great gasp of excitement, and Oliver almost fell off his broomstick in surprise. He swerved around just in time to see Horace gobbling down the pill.

There was a loud whizzing sound, and a bright green flash of light, and Horace vanished from sight.

"Ooooh!" cried the crowd, as if they were watching fireworks.

Then there came a squeak of joy from the Witch Baby down below. "Horace! You small again!"

Oliver peered down to see his sister picking up her spider, who was now a tiny black dot on her palm – and then the crowd burst into cheers and applause.

He'd done it! The antidote had worked!

"The boy's a hero!" someone cried, and everyone cheered again as he came down to land. People crowded around Oliver, congratulating him and shaking his hand. The mayor even gave him a hug!

Oliver beamed, relieved that the crisis
seemed to be over. A team of council
wizards started cutting down the spider-
silk, using special gloves so that it didn't
stick to them. One by one, the wizards
and witches who'd been trapped in the
silk were set free, and everyone began

going about their business again. Well, almost everyone.

Oliver's heart sank as Mrs. Beardbristle stomped over towards them, her mouth set in a grim line. "Your children," she said, stabbing a finger at Mr. Moon, "have been causing trouble ALL DAY. And—"

Mr. Moon glanced at Oliver, then fished in his pocket and took out a packet of what looked like yellow sweeties. "Care for one of these, Mrs. B?" he said politely, opening the bag and holding it out to her. Then he gave Oliver a wink.

"A sweet? I'd say it was the least you could do," she sniffed. She thrust a hand inside and drew out one of the yellow things, unwrapping it and popping it into her mouth. "Did you know what they did this morning, those cheeky little brats of yours? They—"

Then she stopped abruptly. A strange expression came over her face, one that Oliver had never seen before. It was almost like… No, surely it couldn't be. Surely that wasn't a *smile* on his grouchy old neighbour's face, was it?

"What was I saying?" she asked dreamily, bending down to ruffle the Witch Baby's hair.

"Hello, pumpkin. Aren't you adorable?"

"Ooh yes," the Witch Baby agreed. "Me adorable."

Oliver stared in amazement at the change that had come over ferocious Mrs. Beardbristle. Was this some kind of trick? Why was she being so unusually pleasant?

"And dear Oliver, growing up so nicely," she said, patting him on the head and smiling at him. "Anyway, must get on. Goodbye!"

Oliver stared at his dad as Mrs. Beardbristle bustled away down the high street. "What…what just happened?" he asked, bewildered.

Mr. Moon beamed and held up the bag. "These Cure-Alls are brilliant," he replied.

"I bought them for your mum, to cure her flu, but it seems they cure bad tempers, too."

Oliver laughed. To think he'd ever thought this day was going to be boring! "Cool!" he said. "Let's go and give Mum one of the Cure-Alls. If they're strong enough to sort out Mrs. B, they'll make Mum better in no time. The prickleberries should be ready now, too."

Mr. Moon hoisted the Witch Baby back into her baby seat on his broomstick. "Now hold tight to Horace," he instructed her. "And no more spider spells."

She shook her head solemnly. "No more spidey spells," she repeated.

Oliver grinned as he swung his leg over his broomstick. For once, he was *glad* to hear his sister copying something! "Too right, sis," he said. "Let's go home."

And they did.

# The End

# Oliver Moon
# Junior Wizard

## Collect all of Oliver Moon's magical adventures!